MW00444905

Commune-A-Key Publishing
P.O. Box 507
Mount Shasta CA 96067
U.S.A.

(Library of Congress Cataloging in-Publication Data)

Summers, Caryn L.
The girl, the rock, and the water: rediscovering the child within / by Caryn L. Summers
p. cm.
Fictional account of mythic story of personal growth.
Preassigned LCCN: 94-70996.
ISBN 1-881394-19-0

1. Self-actualization. I. Title.

BF637.S4S85 1994 158.1
QBI94-682

Printed and packaged by Palace Press in Hong Kong.
Recorded at Oregon Sound Studios, Medford, OR.
Cover design by Lightbourne Images, Ashland, OR.
Inside pages by Quicksilver Productions, Mt. Shasta, CA.

ISBN 1-881394-19-0 $19.95

the Girl the Rock and the Water

Rediscovering the Child Within

by Caryn Summers, R.N.
Music by Gerry Smida
Illustrated by Ona Le Sassier

Introduction

Since ancient times, storytelling has been a healing art. Stories teach with imagery, sounds and moods. Parables and mythology reach into the heart as well as the mind. Creative stories can be used to open one's heart to feelings and to develop self-awareness. They spark the imagination of the reader and allow self-defeating behaviors, fears of pain, and reactions to stress to be addressed in non-judgmental, poetic verse.

In a storyteller's realm, not far from our own reality, we sometimes find characters and places similar to life's experiences. *The Girl, the Rock and the Water* tells of a child whose safety and dignity have been threatened from abuse, neglect, or addictions.

We find the child at a playground with ferris wheels and games that symbolize her uncontrollable life. The child falls off a merry-go-round and is teased by her friends. She escapes from the chaos, running deep into the desert canyons, in search of a soothing path that will take her away from her shaming, taunting playmates.

Far from home, the child finds an isolated rock that offers her safety and seclusion. Birds join in the chorus of the psalm that is being sung as she bares her soul to the silent rock. There is wisdom that can be found in the red rock. The child learns about a life of quietude and independence. But the human walk is not intended to be one of isolation. The rock cannot substitute for the part of life that requires relating to others.

The girl must leave the rock and travel the waters of emotions and experience. She does this with the assistance and guidance of a white horse.

The characters in the story may remind you of yourself or your acquaintances. The gender of the main character in this story is female, yet her issues of personal travail and subsequent growth apply to either sex.

You need not to have come from a chaotic or upsetting childhood to remember feelings of shame, of not fitting in, or of wanting to run and hide from your peers and loved ones. Indeed, this may have happened to all of us. As you read this story, be aware of situations or characters that arouse feelings in you. Pause at times, listen to the accompanying tape and allow the music, the words and your feelings to soothe your memories and begin the healing process.

A pamphlet with questions and thoughts to ponder is included with the story. You are invited to use this section as a tool to assist you on the journey of surrender, trust and freedom from fear.

Now, with childlike simplicity, please join in the story of *the Girl, the Rock and the Water.*

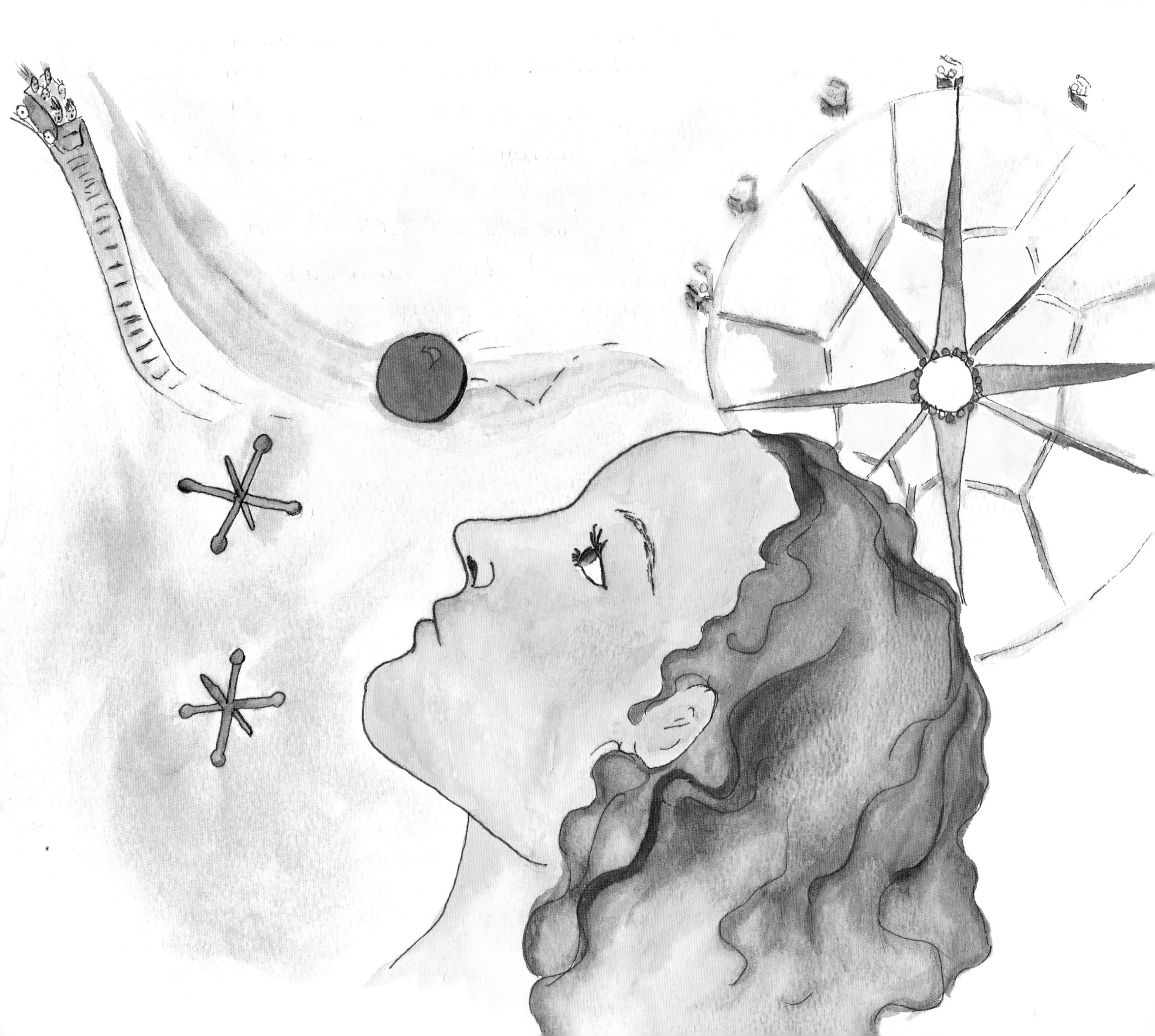

One autumn day, a beautiful woman strolled along the boardwalk of a busy amusement park. Smells of cotton candy and hot dogs carried feelings of nostalgia with them. Music from a nearby ferris wheel and the calls of the many vendors beckoned her back to childhood. Seeing so many people at play caused her heart to ache with a loneliness that she could not understand.

The woman quietly sat down on a park bench and began to watch a group of children as they shouted and jumped onto a merry-go-round. The merry-go-round reminded the woman of her life — so much chaos, spinning round and round, making her feel dizzy and confused.

The woman saw a little girl with curly brown hair and big brown eyes standing alone, separate from the other children. She noticed that the small child was hesitant to join in the play, and she wondered if the child was afraid of falling off, of failing, of becoming embarrassed or hurt. The woman remembered how it felt to desperately want to belong to a group of friends and family that would hold her and love her. She watched the child take a deep breath as she slowly climbed onto the ride.

The merry-go-round went faster and faster, round and round, until the child appeared to be light-headed and dazed. The woman's heart reached out to the child as if she herself were intoxicated by the speed and loss of control.

The woman heard the little girl yell, "Stop, please! I don't like this awful feeling." But the children laughed and went faster. The little girl began to cry. She grabbed tightly to anything she could find to hold on to. But she began to slide off the ride, away from the scary laughter, away from the noise, away from her friends. As she landed painfully on the ground, the children started to tease and laugh at her.

The harsh words of the children stung the woman's heart like a thistle. She felt sadness for the child, for their cruel laughter prevented the girl from enjoying the sweet rose of friendship.

When the child stood up and brushed the sand from her dress, her face was red with disgrace. "I don't need you. I don't need anyone," she whispered as she turned quietly and walked away.

The woman sat on the bench, remembering the time she had walked away from her friends, just like this precious little child. She watched as the girl with big teary eyes left the children and began to climb a windy trail that led up and away from the playground. Where would this child go?

Overhead, a group of black crows cawed in sorrow. The crows reminded the woman of a place in the desert that she once escaped to as a child, a special place of peace and safety where nothing could hurt her.

The woman closed her eyes and began to drift off, into the images of the desert red rock that she remembered so fondly. She felt the journey of the frightened child as if it were her own. And with a breath that ignited her deepest imagination, she became the child with curly brown hair and big brown eyes, slowly making her way into the desert and toward the solitary red rock mountains.....

The secluded mountains called to the child with promises of safety and solitude. "I will hold you through the lonely nights," the child heard the red rock sing to her through the voice of the desert breeze. "You will be protected from the fearful days. You will be safe." She continued to climb, making her way toward the distant pledge of safety and love.

The trail became rocky and difficult to follow. Sticks and stones reached up to scrape her knuckles as she reached for hand-holds to assist her.

But the desert sandstone beneath her feet was warm and inviting, urging the child on. She climbed higher and higher, wandering upward, searching for a quiet retreat, a haven from the painful life below.

As the sun dropped lower into the rosy orange desert sky, an enormous wall of red rock ahead smiled down upon her. The great rock wall cast a tall shadow behind her, pushing her gently forward. The child climbed into the giant rock's waiting arms and she felt protected.

"My child, I have been awaiting your arrival," Grandfather Rock greeted her. "But how did you know I would come?" the child quetioned with uncertainty. She was slow to trust this rock figure, for she had trusted before and had been hurt before.

The red rock smiled and explained, "I listened to the black crows today. They told a sad story of a little girl at the playground who needed to find shelter from the hurt. I am Grandfather Rock, strong and safe. You are welcome here."

Cold and tired, the little girl snuggled into his arms. The mighty red rock held her, asking, "What are you frightened of? What is this pain of childhood that you carry with you?" He quietly listened as the child told him of her shame, her fears, and the confusion in her heart.

Grandfather Rock watched the child's face carefully as she cried. He was fascinated by her tears, for the rock was incapable of crying. He could not feel such emotions as fear, pain or shame. He could not even feel the emotions of happiness, joy or glee. For he was only a rock.

Yet he could love. For love is universal and is not limited to humans. Crows and coyotes can love, clouds and cactus can love, even walls of granite and sandstone can love.

The child became very fond of the gritty old sandstone. As she hugged the mighty red rock she exclaimed, "Oh Grandfather Rock, I feel safe with you. You are truly rugged, yet I know you will not hurt me. Nothing will hurt me while I am here in your arms!"

The little girl with curly brown hair and big brown eyes lay on the desert rock during the long crisp autumn days. The sweet little girl felt warm and cozy in the arms of Grandfather Rock. His broad surface captured the heat of the sun to warm her fragile body.

Grandfather Rock told her the story of the fragile cactus blossom. The child listened carefully as he pointed to a prickly pear cactus on the ledge of the cliff. "The cactus plant is born into the barren soil of the desert," he said. "There is very little to nurture its new life."

She felt sad for the cactus and started to cry.

Grandfather Rock wiped her tears and continued lovingly, "Yet, my child, even with shallow roots and sparse water, this precious cactus brings forth bright pink blossoms of love at a special time each year."

Grandfather Rock sang the child beautiful ballads of the vast desert: songs of the crows, the desert animals, the clouds, and of thunder and lightening in the mystical night sky. The songs of the red rock thrilled her as no music ever had. Sometimes the child would dance, swirling in a solitary motion into the desert dawn. And the child was safe in her dance.

The girl felt like a princess here on the red rock. The scarlet cliffs became her castle and the crimson canyons were her courtyard. Yet she was a princess alone.

There was something that Grandfather Rock could not give this child. Although he could love, he could not offer human companionship. He could not express emotions or feelings. After all, Grandfather Rock's heart was made only of clay.

As the warm autumn days passed by, the rock taught the child how to sit quietly. She learned how to live alone, without merry-go-rounds or chaos. The child was happy to learn these lessons of solitude. She wanted only to be held by Grandfather Rock. "I'm getting stronger!" she would boast to the red rock. "I do not need other children anymore." Grandfather Rock looked at the child with concern, yet said nothing.

At times the child wondered about her family and friends. She missed climbing up on her father's knee to giggle and laugh. Sometimes she even caught a smell riding on the desert breeze that reminded the child of her mother's homemade bread wafting sweet from the kitchen back home.... back home.....

The woman on the park bench awoke from her daydream. She opened her bleary eyes. She was still sitting alone. "Certainly," the woman mused aloud, "if I sit with the wisdom and composure of the sandstone, my loneliness will leave. I, too, will learn how to need only me. I, too, will someday forget my shame, my sorrow and my pain."

But deep in her heart, the woman was troubled. Something was missing. What was it? Was there more than the safety and warmth of Grandfather Rock?

The caw of crows soaring above brought the woman's attention back to the little child. She closed her eyes and turned once again to the red rock in the desert...

The child confided in Grandfather Rock about her troubles – and the rock listened carefully, captivated by her emotions. "I could never go back!" the child exclaimed. Her sadness almost broke this hard rock's protected shell right open.

Grandfather Rock called on his friends, the crows, for an audience to the child's story. The crows cocked their heads and cawed in a sorrowful chorus as the child sang the beautiful and haunting song of a wounded heart. In her song she would beg the rock for the safety of his arms.

After many silent desert days and desolate nights, the child became melancholy. "Child, what is wrong?" the rock asked, concerned for her happiness.

But the child shook her head defiantly and curled up in the rock's strong arms, resisting her loneliness and pain. "Teach me more about the strength in silence. Teach me the survival skills of living alone. Show me how I can collect water from the shallow roots of the desert plants."

Grandfather Rock closed his eyes and said, "There is more for you than survival, my dear. There is happiness waiting for you."

"What do you know of happiness?" the child retorted. "You do fine without it!" And again Grandfather's wall of rock could not protect him from an unfamiliar pang in his heart.

The child did not eat or drink for many days and nights, partaking only of the desert solitude. The warmth of the rock was the only nourishment she received. She became frail and thin.

Grandfather Rock felt the weight of her body lessening. "My dear," he whispered, "you are dying here in my solitary arms."

The brown-eyed girl quickly shook her curls and tried hard to smile. "You, Rock, are all I need. Hold me now, and I will sing to you a song about these soft white clouds. Do not send me back to the chaos of the playground. Here is where I find safety. That's all that I need, no more."

And she sang,

"Hold me, Hold me,
I've never been held before.
Safety, safety,
That's all I need, no more."

The rock sighed softly. "I am only a Windbreak, my child... not a Fortress. I cannot protect you from your heart's inner callings." As Grandfather Rock spoke, a gust of wind wrapped around his shoulders, forming a familiar winter cape. He realized that autumn was ending. He looked down at the child. "Soon even my warm surface of sandstone will be cold. You will need the warmth of family gathered around the fireplace, my child."

Grandfather Rock felt her grip tighten on his tough and weathered surface. He was aware of her fragile and delicate skin – not rough as the sandstone, but soft as human. At that moment the rock's heart of stone broke open and he felt something he had never experienced before. He felt an awesome grief. He would miss her, yet he must send her on her way.

Grandfather Rock called upon the clouds to cry for him – for the strong, isolated red rock could not yet make tears. "Bring the tears I cannot shed!" The vast sky became dark with emotion, stirring into a ferocious desert storm. Again the rock pleaded, lifting his voice upward to the ominous gray clouds, "Cry for me, Clouds! Assist this beloved child on her journey!"

The clouds crashed together and heavy rains drenched the parched and thirsty desert ground. The rock prayed for strength and called again on the clouds to cry even harder, to release torrents of tears. Clouds bellowed, thunder wailed, lightening flashed! The heavens wept for the child and for Grandfather Rock.

The torrents quickly became a great flash flood, swirling around the red rock, creating a rushing and turbulent river. White-caps broke upward through the depths of the tears.

The child called out in fear, "Grandfather Rock! Shelter me from this frightening rain! I have nothing to protect me! These tears falling on my cheeks scare me so! I do not trust this emotion! Let me stay here in safe isolation with you!" The rock quietly bowed his head.

The white-caps in the river leapt high and the child with curly brown hair and big brown eyes gasped. Out of the stormy iridescent waters arose a team of splendid white horses with magnificent manes.

The horses stamped their hooves and flared their nostrils in delightful anticipation. They pranced eagerly and called out to the child in an almighty chorus of infinite love:

"Come with us!
Let go! Let go!
We will help you on your way.

Your heart will heal,
As you learn to feel.
Trust us this special day."

The child shouted out her love to Grandfather Rock. "I trust only you, Grandfather. Tell me, must I truly let go?"

The red rock closed his eyes and slowly nodded yes.

"You are all I need," the child argued in one last attempt to remain in seclusion.

"No, my dear. I am but a stone pillar," said Grandfather Rock, "and you are a human being. I can provide safety whenever you are in danger, but I cannot feed you. And when it's time for you to grow, I cannot teach you all that you must learn. Now, go."

Suddenly something miraculous took place. Grandfather Rock began to cry genuine tears!

As the tears tumbled down Grandfather Rock's face, the rock's surface became slippery – too slippery for the child's soft little hands to grasp.

"My child," Grandfather Rock declared with all his might. "Let go! Learn of life! Learn to accept and trust your friends and family."

"Good bye, Grandfather," the child called. "I shall never forget your wisdom, your warmth and your love."

As she slid down the rock's muddy surface, a crystal of sandstone broke loose. She held it in her hand, marveling at its perfect beauty and radiance.

Grandfather Rock spoke lovingly, "This sandstone crystal is to remind you of your inner strength, sweet child. Use it at times when you are frightened; there will surely be those times on your journey. Now, go!"

She embraced the crystal to her heart, where she would always remember it as a precious gift from Grandfather Rock.

The child climbed atop one proud steed that rose above the other white horses in the water. She settled onto his back and gripped his great mane.

"Welcome!" the horse declared. "Are you ready for your journey?"

The child nodded slowly.

The White Horse tossed his head and reared high with excitement. The child cried out in fear of falling again as she did so long ago from the merry-go-round. She turned back to Grandfather Rock, but could not see him through the rain.

Clutching her crystal of sandstone and praying for strength, she heard Grandfather Rock's voice from within assure her, "I will always be with you, my child. Remember that safety dwells in your heart."

The horse neighed happily, "Now are you ready for your journey?"

"I am ready!" the child exclaimed. "Where are we going?"

The exquisite white horse sang her a song about trust in a power greater than oneself:

"We're going on a journey,
to grow up, strong and free.
You'll learn to trust yourself, my dear.
Be brave, there's more for thee!
Only trust and you will see."

The storm began to clear and it was quiet in the desert once again. Grandfather Rock finally opened his eyes. He had truly wept for the first time, without assistance from the clouds. A smile glistened on his wet surface. For even as Grandfather Rock felt the sorrow of loneliness, he now felt the joy of compassion and selfless love.

And the desert cactus bloomed a bright pink blossom of love on this special day, just as the story promised.

Far away downstream, the child looked forward and summoned an inner strength, calling forth her spirit of adventure.

The White Horse was a skilled traveler and knew the waterways well. They rode straight ahead, into the waters of life. The child rode bravely through both painful and happy memories, through peaceful and sometimes tormenting days, through beautiful and long nights.

The child with curly brown hair and big brown eyes rode her White Horse through the streams and tributaries.

She learned how to maneuver her way through rough white water, holding tightly to the crystal of sandstone that Grandfather Rock had given her.

She learned how to relax and surrender to the flow of the river while still, calm waters rocked her to sleep.

The girl even learned to laugh and play in the thrilling waterfalls, allowing herself to be tossed lightly in the air by the sparkling rapids.

The girl learned many wonderful lessons on that river. She learned to love herself. And when he sensed that she loved herself fully, truly, unconditionally, her friend the White Horse came to the river bank to rest. The girl looked overhead as she heard the loud call of her friends, the black crows, soaring above her.

And as the crows cawed, the beautiful woman found herself once again on the park bench at the playground. She slowly opened her eyes and felt the tears flow down her cheeks. She arose from the park bench and looked up the trail behind the trees.

The woman heard a sweet voice calling from a ledge above. To her surprise, she saw the image of a small child sitting on a shelf of rock, laughing gleefully and waving at her. The woman heard the child call, ***"I'm here! I'm home! I'm safe!"***

The woman waved toward the ledge. The child was not there. Did she really hear a child's voice, or was it the crows who had just returned home for the evening?

She gazed at the beautiful evening sunset that bathed the rocks in vibrant colors and dancing shadows.

The beautiful woman walked away from the playground, that special Autumn Eve, whispering farewell to the child with curly brown hair and big brown eyes.

The Ballad of the Girl, the Rock and the Water

*As her world began to shatter,
and her strength began to fail,
she wandered through the desert
seeking a soothing trail.*

*Her curls would sway as her eyes would search
for a haven from the hurt.
So far from friends and human touch
alone, this little girl.*

*Now the Sandstone beckoned to her,
she climbed to find retreat.
Though stones would scrape her tiny hands,
'twas warm beneath her feet.*

*Hold me – Hold me.
I've never been held before.
Safety – Safety.
That's all I need. No more.*

*So she told the rock her troubles.
It listened to her fears.
The dry and thirsty sandstone
drank up her flowing tears.*

*The rock became her fortress,
her perfect hide-away.
But it could not share a human touch
for its heart was made of clay.*

*"My child," the rock would whisper,
"Our souls are not the same."
"But you are all I need," she cried.
"Don't make me go away."*

*Hold me – Hold me.
I've never been held before.
Safety – Safety.
That's all I need. No more.*

*Soon her memory of all human touch
like her body, grew so thin.
The wind, the sun, and Grandfather Rock
were toughening her skin.*

*Crows circled 'round above the two friends,
who knew their time had come.
Grandfather called the clouds to cry
for waters to travel on.*

*"Go, my child, and journey now,
Take this, a part of me."
And he placed a crystal of Sandstone
in her heart of memory.*

*Hold me – Hold me.
I've never been held before.
Safety – Safety.
Do I dare ask for more?*

*White-caps became great white horses
to carry her away.
and holding tight with all her might
she heard her white horse say,*

*"We're going on a journey,
to grow up, strong and free.
You'll learn to trust yourself, my dear.
Be brave, there's more for thee!"*

*Hold me – Hold me.
I've never been held before.
Safety – Maybe,
I do deserve much more.*

*Hold me – Hold me.
I've never been held before.
Safety – Yes Maybe,
I do deserve much more!*

Dedication

This book is dedicated to the desert where the story began:
Zion National Park.

And to Cedella Daimen Ward, the constant loving reminder of my child within.

Acknowledgments

I want to thank the special people who made this beautiful project possible:

Ona Le Sassier, for her touching and childlike illustrations.
Gerry Smida, for his incredible song writing, soundtrack, and voice.
Douglas York, for his expertise as executive producer.
John Mazzei, for his technical wizardry in co-producing and engineering.
Anton Mizerak, for his assembly and editing work.
Oregon Sound Studio, for a peaceful place to record.
Joan Lucas, for lending her talents in dramatic voice coaching.
Gary Zukav, for his sound effects contribution.
Dana Conant of Quicksilver Productions, for her lovely typesetting.
Nancy Lang, my business partner and friend, for her constant emotional support, and editing talents.
Sharon Lang, for believing in "the Girls."

And thanks to Nancy Walker, who started me on this journey.

TITLE	QTY	TOTAL
Caregiver, Caretaker: From Dysfunctional to Authentic Service in Nursing. by Caryn Summers. Essential reading for helpers who tend to care for others before caring for themselves. $16.95 each.		
Inspirations for Caregivers. A classic selection of inspirational quotes collected by Caryn Summers on the motives and rewards for giving care to others. $8.95 each.		
Inspirations for Caregivers: Music and Words, Volumes I and II. Caryn Summers reads the best quotes from *Inspirations for Caregivers* accompanied by original music by Douglas York. $10.95 each.		
Circle of Health: Recovery Through the Medicine Wheel. by Caryn Summers. This personal growth book combines mythology, symbols, Native American tradition and psychology with twelve-step recovery tools. $12.95 each.		
the Girl, the Rock and the Water. by Caryn Summers. A mythological journey of our inner child to safety, trust and freedom. Read by the author. Includes watercolor illustrations, soundtrack, and workbook. $19.95 each.		
Heart, Humor & Healing. by Patty Wooten, RN. A delightful collection of inspiring, fun-filled and laughter provoking quotes designed to promote healing in the patient as well as the caregiver. $8.95 each.		
SUBTOTAL		
Shipping & handling: $3.00 first book, plus $1.25 for each additional item.		
California residents add 7.25% sales tax.		
TOTAL $ ENCLOSED		

ORDER FORM

Need copies for a friend? You may find books published by Commune-A-Key at your local bookstore, or you may order directly.

Mail this form with your check or money order payable to:

Commune-A-Key Publishing
P.O. Box 507
Mount Shasta, CA 96067
or call
1-800-983-0600

Name ______________________________

Address ______________________________

City ______________ State ______ Zip ______

Phone ______________________________

☐ *Please send me information on other products and seminars.*

Caryn Summers has worked within the nursing profession since 1978. She is currently a writer and speaker, presenting workshops on personal growth topics to caregivers and many others.

Caryn works with the California Board of Registered Nurses' Diversion Program, providing assessment and intervention for chemically impaired nurses in Northern California. She facilitates caregiver support groups and provides private consultation to hospitals, employee assisstant programs, and nursing staffs.

Founder of Commune-A-Key Publishing and Seminars, Caryn offers a unique blend of education, nurturing, fun, and adventure to those who attend her workshops.